THE HUNTED

Titles in Teen Reads:

FAIR GAME
ALAN DURANT

HOME
TOMMY DONBAVAND

KIDNAP
TOMMY DONBAVAND

MAMA BARKFINGERS
CAVAN SCOTT

SITTING TARGET
JOHN TOWNSEND

THE HUNTED
CAVAN SCOTT

THE CORRIDOR
MARK WRIGHT

WORLD WITHOUT WORDS
JONNY ZUCKER

Badger Publishing Limited, Oldmedow Road,
Hardwick Industrial Estate, King's Lynn PE30 4JJ
Telephone: 01438 791037

www.badgerlearning.co.uk

THE HUNTED

CAVAN SCOTT

The Hunted ISBN 978-1-78147-561-4

Text © Cavan Scott 2014
Complete work © Badger Publishing Limited 2014

Publisher: Susan Ross
Senior Editor: Danny Pearson
Copyeditor: Cheryl Lanyon
Designer: Bigtop Design Ltd

2 4 6 8 10 9 7 5 3 1

CHAPTER 1

"BETTER SAFE THAN ..."

It had been a good night. Sally Greaves said goodbye to her friends and opened the door out of the youth club. She gasped as a gust of cold wind stung her cheeks. It was freezing. She looked up and down the high street, watching the cars race by, their exhausts billowing in the air behind them. Dad always told her to walk home along the main road, beneath the yellow glare of the street lamps.

"Better safe than sorry," he'd say.

That was all well and good, but walking back via the high street would add a quarter of an hour to

her journey. In this cold. If she nipped
around the back of the club, jumped over
the wall and walked up the lane, she would
be home in no time.

Sally zipped her coat up to her chin. Her mind
was made up. Besides, Dad would never know.
Shoving her hands into her pockets, she hurried
down the steps and turned into the narrow alley
that ran beside the youth club. She was already
thinking about one of her mum's world-famous
hot chocolates. That would warm her up.

The alley was gloomy, lit only by light that spilled
from the youth club's grimy windows. Someone
should clean those, she thought, although she'd
never suggest it. They'd have her outside with a
bucket of soapy water in a flash. Better to keep
quiet. Besides, she didn't need much light. She'd
been playing around here since she was a kid.

Crossing the small courtyard at the back of the
club, Sally climbed on top of the big, yellow bin
in the corner and hopped over the wall. The

lane was even darker. Too dark. Sally paused for a moment, regretting her decision. Perhaps this wasn't such a good idea. She considered scrambling back into the courtyard before shaking her head.

What are you like? she scolded herself. *Afraid of the dark? You're not a kid!*

Taking a deep breath, she started forwards, striding purposefully past the garages that lined the right-hand side of the lane. She was just being silly. Nothing would happen to her. She was safe. Although she did speed up as she passed the murky little corridors that ran between the garages.

Better safe than…

There was a noise from behind. Running feet, heading towards her. Sally span around, her trainers scraping on the gravel. Her eyes were wide and her heart was beating hard in her chest. Was someone there?

No. The lane was empty. Sally took a step
back, her hands screwed up into fists in her coat
pockets. She waited, but nothing moved in front
of her. It must have been noise travelling from
the next street. One of the other kids heading
home from the club. Even so, it had spooked
her enough to change her mind. Dad was right.
She'd head home along the main road, under the
street lamps. Where she could see things clearly.
Where she could be seen. There was a turning
back onto the high street further on down the
lane. She'd come out by the shops. Might even
get some chips.

Sally turned back the way she had been heading
and screamed as a hand grabbed her arm.

CHAPTER 2

TYLER

The hand pulled Sally into one of the narrow corridors beside the garages.

"Let go of me," she cried out, trying to pull her arm free, but whoever it was had a grip like a vice.

"I'll scream," she warned, "I'll scream so loudly they'll hear me in the club."

A palm closed over her mouth, fingers pressing against her cheek.

"Shhhh," said a voice. "Sally, it's OK. It's me."

With a squeak of fear, Sally pushed her attacker away. This time he let go, stepping back into a narrow beam of moonlight. Sally's eyes went wide as she recognised the face.

"Tyler? What the hell did you do that for?"

The boy in front of her raised his hands. "I'm sorry. I didn't mean to scare you," he said.

Sally pulled the front of her coat straight. "You didn't," she lied, wanting to save face. "I was just surprised, that's all."

At least Tyler looked apologetic, his intense blue eyes full of concern. She hadn't known him long. He'd moved to the area a few months back and started coming to youth club almost immediately. All of the girls had looked up when he'd first walked in. Sally could see why, even though he wasn't her type. Tyler was tall and dark haired with an athletic build. Her best friend, Clara, had asked him if he was a footballer. Tyler had just shaken his head. He never seemed to take much notice of them, kept himself to himself. Sally wondered why he came to youth club at all, if he wasn't going to talk to anyone. Perhaps he just liked being mysterious; thought it made him interesting. Not in her book. Besides, he needed to get out more. He was always as pale as a sheet. Made his light-blue eyes even more startling.

The same light-blue eyes that were staring straight at her.

"Were you followed?" he asked. It was the most he'd ever said to her.

"Followed?" she repeated, confused. "Of course not. I mean, I heard footsteps..."

"Where?"

"Back in the lane," she replied, "but there was no one there."

"Are you sure?" he asked, looking as if he was about to grab her again.

Now, he was scaring her.

"I need to get home," she said, trying to barge past him.

"No, please," Tyler said, raising the palms of his hands again as if to show her that he meant her no harm. "We need your help."

"We?" she asked, wondering who else he was talking about.

Tyler looked over her shoulder into the pitch black of the corridor.

"It's OK," he called out. "She's a friend."

Am I? Sally thought, as she followed Tyler's gaze.

There was someone else there. She shifted back as whoever it was stepped out of the shadows. It was a boy, no more than eight or nine. A mop of unruly ginger hair sat above a slightly podgy, dirty face. Why was Tyler hanging around with a kid? It couldn't be his brother. They looked nothing like each other.

"This is Ben," Tyler said, as if he'd read her mind. "He's a friend of the family."

Sally had never heard Tyler mention his family before. Then again, she'd hardly ever heard him speak. She had to admit he had a nice voice. It was surprisingly gentle with some kind of accent. Irish, maybe? There was a slight waver when he spoke, though. As if he was nervous. No, more than that. As if he was scared.

Ben walked cautiously towards Tyler, never taking his eyes off Sally. She looked back at Tyler.

"What's going on?" she asked. "What are you doing out here?"

"Hiding," Ben said, sniffing. It sounded like he'd been crying. Sally couldn't be sure in this light.

"Who from?" she asked.

Tyler looked from his young friend to Sally and sighed. "From the men who are trying to kill us."

CHAPTER 3

RUNNING SCARED

Sally laughed. This had to be a joke. "Yeah, nice try. Hallowe'en isn't until the end of the month."

She pushed past him, annoyed with herself for listening to his nonsense for this long. Not looking back, she marched across the lane, arms crossed tightly across her chest.

"No, wait," Tyler called out. He followed her over to the alleyway that led out to the high street, Ben close behind. "We need your help."

"You need help, all right," she snapped back. "You're not right in the head, you."

She hurried out to the main road, more eager to get home than ever.

Tyler was running now, reaching out for her as she stepped onto the pavement. He grabbed her hand, spinning her around to face him.

"Let go of me," she screamed.

"I'm serious," he urged, squeezing her arm. "They've already tried once tonight. Ben only just got away with his life. You need to help us, please!"

Sally tried to shrug him off. "I don't need to do anything. Let go!"

Tyler's grip was as strong as before. She couldn't wriggle free. Behind Tyler, Ben pulled at his arm, pleading with him to get back in the lane, telling him it wasn't safe.

Out of the corner of her eye, Sally spotted lights moving towards her. She turned to see a car driving in their direction. A big, red car. Twisting in Tyler's grip, Sally waved frantically in the air.

"Hey," she shouted towards the car. "Help me!"

"Sally, no," Tyler hissed in her ear.

Sally kept on yelling. "This creep won't let me go. Help!"

The car swerved in the road. Yes! They'd spotted her. They were going to stop. All at once, Tyler tried to pull her back down the alley, away from the main road. Sally fought back, trying to pull his hand from her arm. She turned to shout to the driver again, but her eyes went wide. The car was still heading towards them, but it wasn't slowing. If anything, it was speeding up. It was going to hit them!

"Sally, move!" Tyler cried out as he yanked her out of the way. The car veered onto the pavement, screaming past them, before slamming on its brakes.

"Run!" Tyler instructed, pulling Sally behind him.

"They tried to run us over!" Sally gasped in shock.

"Yes. I told you," Tyler said, pulling her round into the lane. "They want to kill us and they don't care who gets hurt."

Sally could hear car doors opening and slamming, booted footsteps running down the alley. She glanced over her shoulder to see three large men barrelling into the alley, running full pelt towards them. She didn't need Tyler to pull her along now. She was running for her life and she knew it.

"Where's Ben?" she called out, suddenly realising that he wasn't ahead of them. She looked back to see the boy running behind, but not fast enough.

"They're going to get him," she said, grabbing for Tyler.

"He'll be OK," he replied. "Ben's quick. He can outrun anyone."

There was a cry from behind. It was Ben. He'd tripped, was sprawled on the floor.

"Ben!" Sally shouted, but it was already too late. The men were upon him in an instant. Ben tried to scrabble to his feet, but was grabbed by one of the men, a big brute with a completely bald head and a scar running down his face.

The man pulled Ben to his feet, blocking his desperate punches.

"We've got to help him," said Sally, starting to run back, but Tyler put out a hand to stop her.

"No," he said, firmly. "It's no good."

"We can't just leave him," she shrieked.

"We've got to," Tyler insisted. "Come on!"

Sally fought against him, just as another of the men struck something against Ben's chest. She screamed the boy's name as he cried out in pain, his body going rigid – but her scream was cut short as brilliant white light burst out of Ben's open mouth, out of his eyes, his ears. Sally raised a hand to shield her eyes as Ben's entire body erupted into a burst of blinding light, illuminating the entire lane.

Sally blinked as the light dimmed. Ben had completely disappeared. All that was left were his clothes. His jacket was still clenched in the bald man's hands, his T-shirt and jeans falling to the floor.

"W-what happened to him?" she stammered, as Tyler tried to pull her back. The bald man looked up towards them and, throwing Ben's jacket aside, starting running straight for them.

CHAPTER 4

A HIDING PLACE

Sally didn't ask any more questions. She ran with Tyler, bolting out of the lane and across a street. She didn't know where they were heading, just knew that they had to get away. She didn't want whatever had happened to Ben to happen to her.

Tyler led the way, cutting down back alleys, helping her jump over fences. They were in a row of back gardens now, scrambling over hedges and walls. Behind one of the houses, an old lady knocked angrily on a kitchen window, telling them to get out of her garden. They did as they were told. They didn't want to stop. They had to keep one step ahead of the men.

Finally, Sally recognised where they were. As she swung herself over the last garden wall, she spotted her old primary school ahead of her. They could hide in there. She grabbed Tyler's hand and pulled him across the road in front of the school.

"Down there," she said, pointing to the caretaker's house. "There's a gap in the fence along the side. We can hide behind the bike sheds."

As long as they haven't fixed it, she thought to herself glumly as they scooted around the side of the house.

They were in luck. The gap was still there, although it was a lot smaller than she remembered. She made it, scraping her cheek against the metal, although Tyler got stuck. She grabbed his arm and pulled, the leather of his jacket squealing as he finally slipped through the gap.

"This way," she said, guiding him along the side of the main school building. It had been years since she'd been there, but she remembered the way as if it was yesterday. Their feet scuffed against the paving slabs as she pulled Tyler into the tight gap between the bike shed and the school wall.

They came to a stop, hardly daring to breathe. Sally strained to listen to the sounds of the night. Once or twice she thought she heard the men's footsteps, but there was nothing. Had they lost them? They waited for a full five minutes, although it seemed forever. Sally realised that she was still holding Tyler's hand. It was freezing. Tyler was trembling, but so was she. She had never been so scared.

"Have they given up?" she whispered, finally breaking the silence.

"They never give up," Tyler replied flatly.

She let go of his hand, struggling to turn to him in the cramped space. "Who are they?" she asked. "Really."

Tyler closed his eyes and let his head fall back against the wall. "They've been after us for years," he admitted quietly.

"You and Ben?"

"The entire family," Tyler said. "They've killed everyone. My mum. My dad. I'm the only one left."

Sally's eyes widened as Tyler told his story. "Why haven't you gone to the police?"

Tyler let out a short, sharp laugh. "The police are in on it. If I went to them, they'd just hand me over. I'd be dead as well."

Sally reached out and touched his arm. "But what did they do to Ben? What was that light?"

Tyler opened his eyes and turned to her. He looked so tired. "That's how they do it. Your body explodes into light. There's nothing left, except for your clothes."

"But how?"

Tyler shrugged. "I don't know. They're monsters. Nothing more."

He placed his hand over hers. His cold, cold hand. "I'm sorry I got you into this," he said, his voice barely audible.

She squeezed his arm. "It's fine. We'll put a stop to this, I promise."

He shook his head. "You can't. It's pointless."

Sally pulled her hand away. She wasn't going to have that. Once she set her mind to something, she saw it through. Had always been the same.

"I'll take you back to my place," she said, a plan forming in her head.

"Yours?"

"We'll talk to Dad," she said. "He'll know what to do. He'll help you."

Tyler took a step away.

"No. I can't endanger your family. It's not fair."

Sally frowned. "I can't let you face this on your own."

She held out her hand, waiting to see if Tyler would take it. She wasn't going to force him. It had to be his choice. The two stood in silence until, finally, he took her hand and smiled. It was a nice smile. Matched his voice, somehow.

Without another word, Sally led them out from behind the shed. They ran back over to the fence and squeezed through. Tyler didn't get stuck this time. Sally poked her head around the corner of the caretaker's house.

"There's no one around," she said, before quickly stepping back into the shadows.

"What is it?" Tyler whispered, his grip on her hand increasing.

She looked again and sighed. She had spotted someone down the end of the road, but it wasn't the men.

"It's nothing," she said. "Just Mrs George from the newsagent walking her dog."

She pulled at his hand. "Come on. Let's get you home."

*

Sally's heart was pounding all the way home. They didn't speak, but kept looking nervously up and down the road. Every approaching car made her breath catch in her throat. Would the driver try to mow them down? She only allowed herself to breathe once the car had safely passed by. They didn't take the high street, keeping to the back roads. Dad wouldn't like it, but the main road hadn't been very safe, had it? Eventually, they jogged down the hill leading to her road, still hand in hand.

"My house is just around here," Sally said, flashing a relieved smile at Tyler. "Number 62."

She was starting to round the corner, when Tyler hissed in her ear.

"Wait," he said, pulling her back.

"What now?" Sally asked.

"There," Tyler said, pointing across the road. "Is that your dad?"

Sally looked across at her house. The door was open, light spilling onto the front drive.

"Yeah, that's him." Her eyes narrowed. "Who's he talking to?"

Her blood ran cold. Dad was talking to two
men, one bald, one with thin, brown hair.
Her eyes flicked to the third man, sitting in
the driver's seat of the red car parked outside
her house.

"The men from the lane," she gasped, covering
her mouth with her free hand. "What are they
doing here?"

CHAPTER 5

NO PLACE LIKE HOME

Sally watched in horror as her dad talked to the men. One of them reached inside his jacket and pulled out a piece of paper. No, it was a photograph. Her dad took it, looked at the picture and shook his head.

"They've got to him," whispered Tyler, trying to pull her back up the hill. "They're after you, too, now. Because of me."

Sally tried to stop him. "No. Dad wouldn't help them." The thought of it was making her feel sick.

Tyler gazed at her with those brilliant blue eyes. "They're clever. They know what to say to make people do what they want. He won't have a choice."

Tears pricked Sally's eyes. "But he wouldn't hand me over," she insisted.

"Sally, if you go back, they'll hurt him too. Maybe worse."

Sally imagined her dad struggling with the men – the flash of light, his clothes lying discarded on the floor.

Tyler was still speaking. "We need to find somewhere else to go."

Sally thought of something. "My grandad. He lives near here. He'll help us."

Tyler shook his head. "No. It's too dangerous."

Behind them, they heard the doors of the men's car slamming. The engine starting.

"We've got to get out of here," Tyler said.

"I've got it," Sally said. "Grandad has a garage round the back of his house. Uses it to store all kinds of junk. We can hide there until we work out what to do."

"Is it locked?" Tyler asked, his eyes flicking nervously to the end of the road. The car's headlights had switched on.

"I know where he keeps the key," Sally said, pulling on his arm. "It won't take long."

*

The garage was only three streets away. Sally left Tyler hiding behind a skip and ran to her grandad's bungalow, across the other side of the playing field. She had to fight the urge to knock on his door and ask him to help. Tyler was right. It was too dangerous. They would be safe in the garage. They could spend the night there and work out what to do next.

Trying not to make a noise, she opened the side gate to her grandad's garden, wincing as the hinges squeaked. She froze, waiting to see if the old man would come out to investigate. There was no sound from inside the bungalow. He must be asleep. Grandad always went to bed early in the autumn.

She crept down to where he kept his bins and felt around for the flowerpots down by the wheels. She touched something slimy and snatched her hand back. Yuck! Must have been a slug. Shuddering with disgust, she tried again, finding the flowerpots this time. Quickly, she checked underneath them one by one. Where was the key? Grandad always hid it beneath one of these.

She lifted the last pot and sighed in relief when her fingers brushed against cold metal. There they were! But there was no time to celebrate. Sally heard a car driving up the road – a car travelling very slowly. Her head snapped around and she saw headlights on the road on the other side of the garden gate. Moving quickly, she ran over to the gate, shutting it as quickly as she dared. The hinges shrieked once again. She crouched behind the gate, listening, as the car drove past. Its tyres crunched on the tarmac. Was it the men? The monsters that were after Tyler?

Sally closed her eyes, willing the car to keep moving. It sounded as if it was stopping, just on the other side of the gate. What if they'd seen it shut? What if they'd heard the hinges squeak?

On the other side of the gate, the car came to a halt with a clunk of brakes. A door opened and someone stepped onto the pavement, just a few metres from where she was hiding.

They'd found her!

CHAPTER 6

SHELTER FOR THE NIGHT

Sally didn't know what to do. Should she make a run for it? Should she try to get around to Grandad's garden and get over the wall? Another car door was opening now.

She put her weight against the gate, wrapping her fingers around the handle. She didn't know if it would make any difference. The men were big, really big. If they tried to barge the gate open, she wouldn't be able to stop them.

Then she heard a laugh. A woman's laugh. The car door slammed shut, followed by the beep of a remote-control lock. The woman was talking now, high-heels clattering on the pavement. There was another set of footsteps too. A man's, but they weren't making for the gate. They were walking down the road, away from her.

Sally let herself relax. It must just have been one of Grandad's neighbours, coming home after a night out. Sally felt like laughing herself as she listened to the footsteps fade away. She heard keys being jangled, then turned in a lock. A front door opened, the woman laughed again, and it slammed shut.

The road was silent once more.

Sally waited for a minute and then opened the gate and peered outside. She needed to get back to Tyler.

*

The pale-skinned boy was waiting where Sally had left him, sitting behind the skip, his knees pulled close to his chest. She thought he was going to hug her when he saw her, but he stopped himself. She was glad. She still didn't know what she felt about him and didn't want him to get the wrong idea, nice voice or not.

She beckoned Tyler over to her grandad's garage, the newly painted green doors glinting in the light of a solitary street lamp. At least she would be able to see the padlock. She'd had enough of scrabbling around in the dark.

The key stuck as she pushed it into the lock, but slipped into place as she wiggled it. She turned it once, but the padlock wouldn't budge. She tried again. The same thing.

"Here," said Tyler, "Let me."

She stepped aside, letting him bend down to take the key. The padlock sprang open on his second attempt, the sound surprisingly loud in the night air.

Sally shook her head. "I'm too jumpy," she sighed, running a hand through her short, black hair.

Tyler smiled grimly. "It's understandable."

He reached down and yanked at the garage door. It started to swing up, making even more noise than her grandad's gate. Tyler stopped it before it was half-way up and Sally ducked underneath.

She went straight for the shelves where she knew her grandad kept his torches. There was an old paraffin camping lamp and a big orange torch with a rubberised grip. Not expecting it to work, Sally turned the dial on the side of the lamp. The garage was immediately bathed in a warm, orange glow. The lamp still had gas in it. Good old Grandad.

She nodded for Tyler to come inside and pull the door shut. He did so, the closing mechanism complaining nosily. When it was shut, Sally walked over and threw a bolt on the inside of the door.

They were safe, for now.

CHAPTER 7

CAUGHT

Sally didn't sleep much that night. She found a couple of old blankets in a cardboard box and Tyler made a makeshift bed against the back wall, using old newspapers. It looked like he'd done it before.

He'd told her to take the bed. He'd sleep at the front, next to the door.

"Just in case," he'd said gravely.

She'd lain awake, listening for the sound of cars searching the street. When she had drifted off to sleep, her dreams were full of blinding, white flashes.

Morning came and she pushed herself up from the now scattered newspaper. Her back ached terribly. Concrete floors were not comfortable places to sleep. Tyler was already awake, sitting on a stool, his ear to the metal door.

"Are you hungry?" she asked.

Tyler nodded. "Starving. Haven't had a bite for days."

Sally frowned. "Where have you been hiding?"

He shrugged. "Wherever we could find. Ben was always good at finding hiding places." A look of sadness swept over his white face.

Sally pulled up the zip of her coat and glanced over to one of her grandad's workbenches. A dark blue beanie hat was thrown on top of one of the boxes. She'd bought it for him two Christmasses ago, to keep him warm when he worked in the garden. He'd never liked it. Said it was too young for him. She walked over and picked it up, feeling the fabric between her fingers. It would do for now. Besides, her hair must look a right state. She pulled it over her head.

"How do I look?" she said, turning to Tyler.

He smiled, a little weakly. "Very stylish."

"I'm going to find us some food. We can decide what we'll do when I get back. What do you fancy?"

Tyler shook his head. "I don't know. Surprise me."

"I think we've had enough surprises for one night," she said, pulling back the bolt on the door.

*

She wasn't gone long. It was hot in her grandad's hat, but she didn't take it off. Didn't want to be recognised. She purposely went to a different shop from usual, grabbing some crisps and chocolate bars. Hardly the healthiest breakfast, but this was hardly a usual morning. When she got back to the garage, she knocked three times on the door.

"It's me," she said, trying to keep her voice as quiet as possible. She heard the bolt sliding across and pulled the door up high enough to duck beneath.

Once the door was shut again, she gladly yanked the beanie from her head and threw it back on the box. She pulled out a chocolate bar and offered it to Tyler.

"Here you go."

He shook his head. "I'm not hungry."

"But you said you hadn't eaten in days."

He stalked back to his stool. "Seriously. I couldn't."

Sally looked at the chocolate bar. She was nervous too, but her stomach was rumbling.

"Suit yourself." She ripped the top of the wrapper and took a bite. It tasted wonderful.

She was just about to ask Tyler if he'd had any ideas about what to do next, when someone tried the handle to the garage door.

Tyler leapt from his seat. "Sally! The bolt."

Sally spun around. She'd forgotten to lock the door. Stupid, stupid girl. She grabbed for the lock, but the door was already swinging open.

"Get back," Tyler cried, suddenly in front of her.

How had he moved so quickly? She dropped her chocolate bar as he bustled to the back of the garage, pushing her behind a pile of boxes covered in an old tarpaulin. Sunlight streamed into the front of the garage and they heard three sets of feet step in.

Sally peeked through a gap, her eyes widening as she saw the bald man from the night before. He was even bigger than she remembered, with blunt features. His nose looked as if it had been broken at some point in the past. He stopped, hands thrust into his jacket pockets, piggy eyes scanning the garage. They came upon the chocolate bar and he bent to pick it up.

Behind him, the man with the brown hair spoke up. "I know you're in here," he said in a thin voice. "There's nowhere to hide now."

The bald man joined in. "We know you took the girl. Don't make it worse for yourself."

Sally didn't know what to do. She stared back at Tyler, who was glaring at the men through gaps in the tarpaulin. His mouth was a thin, straight line. His cheeks even paler than ever.

Then he did something Sally didn't expect. He stood up, hooking a hand under Sally's arm, pulling her with him.

In front of them, the bald man stood at the same time.

"Yeah," Tyler said. "I took the girl. You tried to kill her, remember?"

Sally winced. Tyler's fingers were digging into her arm, holding her tightly. Too tightly.

"Have you hurt her?" the brown-haired man asked, his eyes looking Sally up and down.

"No," Tyler said. "She helped me."

"Then let her go," said the third man who was standing at the back of the trio.

"Why?" asked Sally, surprised to hear her own voice. She'd meant to stay quiet, but couldn't help herself. "So you can make me disappear like you did Ben?"

The bald man pointed a stubby finger at her. "Stay out of this," he warned. "You don't know what's happening."

"I know you're monsters," Sally blurted out.

The brown-haired man laughed. "Is that what he's told you?"

Now that Sally had started talking she couldn't stop. "He told me you killed his family. Murdered his mum and dad."

"Lies," the bald man sneered. "All lies. We didn't kill his family. Tyler did."

It was Sally's turn to laugh. "I don't believe you. You'd say anything to get to us." She turned to Tyler. "That's right, isn't it?"

Tyler didn't answer. Instead, he sighed and looked down at his feet.

"I'm sorry, Sally, but they're right."

Sally couldn't believe what she was hearing. She tried to pull away, but Tyler held her tight.

"I did kill my dear old mum and dad. A lifetime ago. And I'm going to kill you, if they don't let me go."

When Tyler looked up, his eyes weren't blue any more. They were as black as night, but that wasn't why Sally started screaming. She started screaming because of the large, white fangs gleaming in Tyler's open mouth.

CHAPTER 8

THE TRUTH

She had been tricked. The men weren't monsters. Tyler was the monster. He was a vampire, as crazy as that sounded. He lunged forwards, pulling her close. She could smell his breath, rotten, like meat gone bad. She pushed against him, never taking her eyes from those razor-sharp teeth.

Thinking quickly, she reached out with her free hand, pulling at the old tarpaulin. She threw it back over Tyler, covering him. He bellowed in fury, his fingers digging into her arm. She cried out in pain, and suddenly the bald man was rushing forwards. He grabbed at Tyler through the tarpaulin, but the vampire merely threw up an arm. It was as if he had swatted a fly. The large man was knocked across the garage, crashing into a set of shelves. Pots of paint tumbled down, spilling their multi-coloured contents on the back of the vampire hunter.

The noise was deafening in the enclosed space, but it was the distraction Sally needed. She pushed against Tyler, still struggling to shrug off the tarpaulin. He stumbled, tripping over her grandad's boxes, and fell forwards, letting go of her arm.

"No," he cried out, landing in a heap on the floor. He writhed under the heavy sheet, finally throwing it from him. Then he started screaming. Tyler was caught in a beam of sunlight that streamed through the open door. Sally covered her mouth as his pale skin started to steam, blisters bubbling over his face. He twisted on the floor, trying to scramble back into the shadow at the back of the garage, but the brown-haired man leapt forwards. He raised an arm and rammed something into Tyler's back with a dull thud.

Tyler bellowed in pain, light blazing from his open mouth. Sally screwed her eyes shut, knowing what was coming. There was a sound like a thousand light bulbs shattering at once, the sudden flare visible even through her eyelids.

When she opened them again, Tyler was gone, leaving nothing more than a pile of clothes and a wooden stake on the floor. The brown-haired man picked up his stake, wiping the wood against his long coat. She felt his eyes upon her.

"Are you OK?" he asked.

"I didn't know," she stammered, her body starting to shake uncontrollably from the shock.

"We've been chasing Tyler for a long time," the man said. "A very long time. You sure he didn't hurt you?"

Sally shook her head, suddenly wanting to go home more than anything in the whole world.

"He was probably keeping you in case we caught up with you," the man explained, slipping his weapon back into his pocket. "A bargaining chip. Still, we should get you checked out by a doctor before we take you home, just in case."

He held out an arm. Still trembling, Sally stepped out from behind the junk, allowing him to guide her around Tyler's crumpled clothes.

"That's it," the vampire hunter said. "Better safe than sorry."

THE END